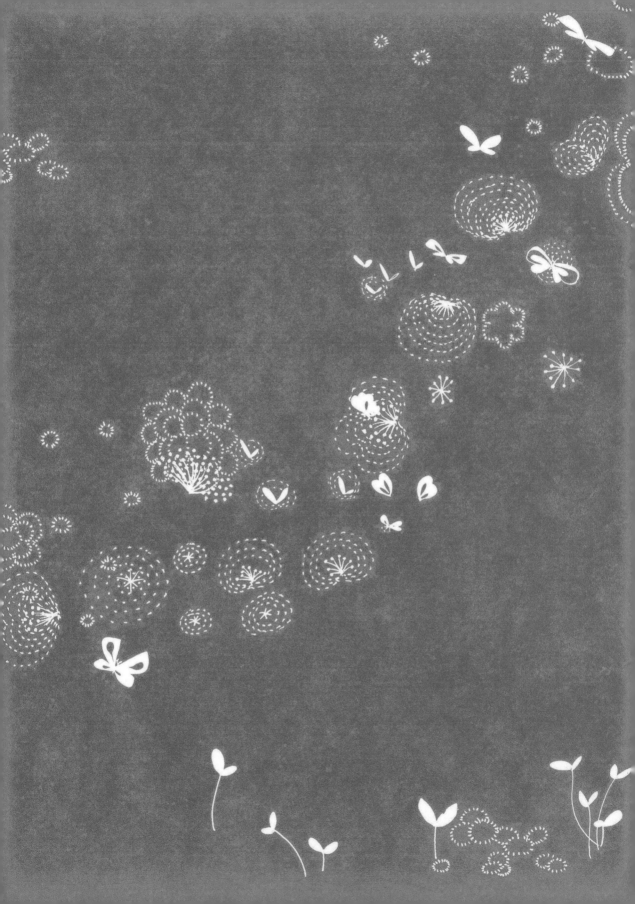

For Eleanor and Cara Shearer, with love from the donkey ~
JW
For Kyriacos ~
RM

First published in 2009 by Scholastic Children's Books
This edition first published in 2011 by Scholastic Children's Books
Euston House, 24 Eversholt Street
London NW1 1DB
a division of Scholastic Ltd
www.scholastic.co.uk
London ~ New York ~ Toronto ~ Sydney ~ Auckland
Mexico City ~ New Delhi ~ Hong Kong

Text first published in 2007 in *The Times*
Text copyright © 2007 and 2009 Jeanette Winterson
Illustrations copyright © 2009 Rosalind MacCurrach

978 1407 10905 3

1 3 5 7 9 10 8 6 4 2

The moral rights of Jeanette Winterson and Rosalind MacCurrach have been asserted.

Papers used by Scholastic Children's Books are made from wood grown in sustainable forests.

The Lion, the Unicorn and Me

The Donkey's Christmas Story

Jeanette Winterson

Illustrated by Rosalind MacCurrach

SCHOLASTIC

Before it happened, an angel lined up all the animals – every one, of every kind, because this angel had the full list left over from the Ark.

Most were eliminated at once – spiders, monkeys, bears, whales, walruses, snakes. Soon it was clear that four legs on the ground at the same time would be necessary to reach the qualifying round. That left some serious competition – horses, tigers, a stag with antlers that branched into an unknown forest, a zebra painted black and white like an argument.

The elephant could carry the world on its back. Dogs and cats were too small, the hippopotamus too wayward. There was a giraffe in jigsaw graffiti. The camel was wanted elsewhere, as were the cattle. After a long time, it was just the three of us: the lion, the unicorn and me.

The lion spoke first. Present position: King
of the Jungle. Previous history: worked with
Hercules and Samson, also Daniel in
the lions' den. Special strengths: special
strength. Weaknesses: none reported. The
angel wrote it down.

Then the unicorn spoke. Present position:
mythical beast. Previous history: in Hebrew
I am Re'em, the creature that cannot be
tamed. Special strengths: known to be good
with virgins. Weaknesses: tendency to vanish.
The angel wrote it down.

Then it was my turn.

"He'll make an ass of himself," whispered the lion. I did. I am. A proper ass. Present position: under-donkey. Previous history: small under-donkey. Special strength: can carry anything anywhere. Weaknesses: not beautiful, not well-bred, not important, not clever, not noticed, not won any prizes...

The angel wrote it down, and down, and down. Then the angel gave us a tie-breaker: could we say, in one sentence, why we were right for the job?

The lion spoke first. "If He is to be King of the World, He should be carried by the King of the Beasts." The unicorn said, "If He is to be the Mystery of the World, He should be carried by the most mysterious of us all."

I said, "Well, if He is to bear the burdens of
the world, He had better be carried by me."

And that is how I found myself trotting
quietly along, the red desert under my hooves,
the sky rolled out like a black cloth over my
head, and a tired woman nodding asleep
on my back, towards the little town
of Bethlehem.

Oh but it was a musty, rusty, fusty pudding of a town turned out for a show, its people cussed and blustering, all buy and sell and money, taking their chance while the going was good before the goods got going again. Taxes, and everyone here to pay up, and everyone had to be put up for this one night, so that even the mice were renting their mouse-holes, and there were travellers hanging out of birds' nests, their beards full of twigs and old worms, and the anthills were full up, and the beehives had three families apiece, and there was a man tapping on the frozen lake asking the fish to let him in.

And every bed and every under-the-bed, and every chair and cushion and curtain and carpet, and every ledge, nook, shelf, cranny, gap, rack, cupboard and cart squeezed and popped with arms and legs. When we arrived at the inn, there were two large, empty pots on either side of the door.

Being a donkey, I poked my head into one of them to see if there was anything to eat. At once, a stubbly face popped out of the pot, and warned us that the inn was so full that he and his brother had had to uproot the olive trees from either side of the porch. Sure enough, there was the brother, head like a melon, scowling in the other pot.

My master Joseph was an optimistic man. He knocked at the door. The innkeeper opened it, and the boy who had been sleeping in the letterbox fell out.

"No room," said the innkeeper.

"For my wife only?" asked Joseph. "Tonight she will bear a Son."

"Then she must do it by starlight," said the innkeeper, closing the door. Joseph put his foot in the way.

"Listen," said the innkeeper, "you think I'm joking?" He pointed upwards, into the beams, where five spiders were looking gloomily at six infants whose father had knotted the webs into hammocks.

Joseph nodded and was about to turn away, when the innkeeper said, "But go round the back to the stables, and see what you can find." Now, the animals that night knew that something strange was going to happen because animals always do know when something strange is going to happen.

They were murmuring among themselves: the ox had seen a star glowing brighter and brighter, and the camel had had a message from his brother, who worked for a king, that kings were travelling to Bethlehem that night.

The sheep who loved their shepherds had been lying quietly in the frost-filled fields when a creature bright as hope and fast as chance had de-frosted the ground where he stood, and told of a birth to come.

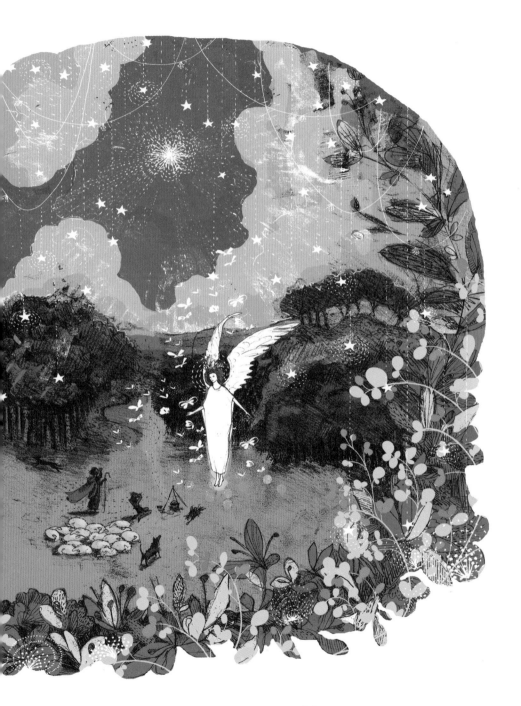

Mary, Joseph and me pushed our way into
the crowded stable. It smelled of sweet, warm
dung and dry hay. I was hungry. Straight away,
Joseph swept some straw into a heap, and
spread out a blanket from the saddlebags.
He went outside to fill his leather bottle with
water from the well, and because he was a
kind man, he brought in fresh water for the
hot, crowded animals too. Mary was glad of
the heat of the animals. She fell asleep
for a while.

When I was unsaddled of all my burdens,
Joseph turned me out into the yard to eat
my supper. It was cold, sharp, biting weather.
The stars were bright as bells. The deep black
sky had the new moon cut in it and the fields
beyond the town were visible under that moon,
but as a dream is visible to one who sleeps,
and not to one who is awake.

"Something will happen tonight," said
the ox. "I can feel it in my shoulders."

"I can smell it," said the dog.

"It's quivering my whiskers," said the cat.
The horse pricked her ears and looked up.
I carried on eating because I was hungry.
Eating as only an ass can eat, I saw the light
flash across my hooves, and wipe from grey to
bright the turned-over, trampled and frosted
clods of earth around the stable. I looked up;
the back of the inn was ramshackle and dark,
but the stable was shining. Two creatures in
bright array were sitting on the slipped clay
tiles of the ridge, their feet clean and bare,
their hair flowing like a fast river, and each
carried a long trumpet slung across his back.

Above them was a star whose edge was so close I thought it would cut the roof in half, and wedge its brightness in the wormy purlins, so that the stable and its star would be solid together, hay and dung and another world.

There was a great commotion, and three
camels, jewelled and brushed, stood steaming
in the yard. At a word, the camels bent and
kneeled, and the kings who rode them each
unpacked a precious box of great price.

In all of this light and motion, I trotted quietly through the little door and pushed my way through the other animals to where Joseph was kneeling beside Mary. She was on all fours, just like us. There was a rushing sound, like water, and a cry, like life.

It was life, bloody and raw, and wet and
steaming in the cold like our breath, and the
Baby, its face screwed up and its eyes closed,
and Joseph's hand bigger than its back, and
suddenly there was the blast of trumpets,
and the front blew clean off the stable, and
I looked up and saw the angels' feet pushed
through the sagging roof and their bodies taut
on the ridge-line, heralding the beginning of
something, the end of something, I don't know
what words to say, but beginnings and ends are
hinged together and folded back against each
other, like shutters, like angels' wings.

I tipped back my head, and I brayed and brayed to join the trumpets. My nose was so high and the roof so low, that the angel's foot brushed me as I sang.

The kings came inside even though there was no inside left now that we were blown inside out, time past and future roaring round us like a wind, and eternity sitting above us, like angels, like a star. The kings kneeled and one of them, the youngest, began to cry.

Then four shepherds, dressed in sheepskins and smelling of sheep dip, came with hot mutton in a broth and poured it into wooden bowls, and Joseph fed Mary as she leaned against him, the Baby under her cloak, Its body lighting up her body, so that even in the gold that was the angels, and the silver that was all the stars of the sky, the Baby shone brighter. They wiped Him. They wrapped Him up. They laid Him in the manger.

Sometime in the night, the lion on soft paws crept in and bowed his head. Sometime in the night, through a gap in the wall, no bigger than thought, the unicorn touched the Baby with his horn.

Morning came, a stretching, yawning, sniffing, snorting, shuffling sort of a morning. I trotted round to the front of the inn, and there were the scowling melon-heads sitting on their pots by the porch, drinking thick coffee from tin cups.

"Look at that donkey's nose," said one.

"What's he been eating?" said the other. I squinted down the velvety barrel of my nose, but I couldn't see anything strange.

All around, the town was waking, merchants and herdsmen, camel-drivers and bankers, and the whispering news was that something wonderful was happening.

The innkeeper came out of the inn. He was the first with the news: King Herod was coming to Bethlehem – what an honour, what a compliment, that must be the meaning of the star, and the babbling portent of the raving drunk asleep in the empty wine barrel – angels on the stable roof, he'd said. He looked at me.

"What happened to your nose?"

The three kings had left before dawn, warned in a fitful dream to return by another route. I had seen their dromedaries moving like music out to the fields where the shepherds were already lighting their morning fire.

There was nothing to show for the night just gone, except three boxes of precious stuff, a hole in the roof where the angels had dangled their feet on the rim of time, and the fact that the stable door had been blown off. Joseph paid for the door with a piece of gold from the box, and showed the innkeeper the Baby Boy, and they talked about the star seen in the East, and the innkeeper gave his opinion, boasting about Herod, and some fool-talk about angels, and then I trotted back round the corner, nose-first.

"Well I'll be blowed," said Joseph.

The truth is that when the angel's foot had
rested on my muzzle as I brayed, my muzzle
had turned as gold as a trumpet that proclaims
another world.

We didn't wait for Herod. We set out for
Egypt, not telling anyone where we had gone,
and I carried Mary and her Baby, many days
and nights, into safety.

Sometimes, when the sky is very cold and
clear, and I have done my day's journey and
stand half-asleep, half-awake in the warmth of
my stall, I think I see the bowl of a trumpet,
and its long funnel, and a foot, clean and white,
dangling over the ridge-line of the stars,
and I lift up my voice and I bray and I bray,
for memory, for celebration, for warning, for
chance, for everything that is here below and
all that is hidden elsewhere. Hay and dung
and another world.

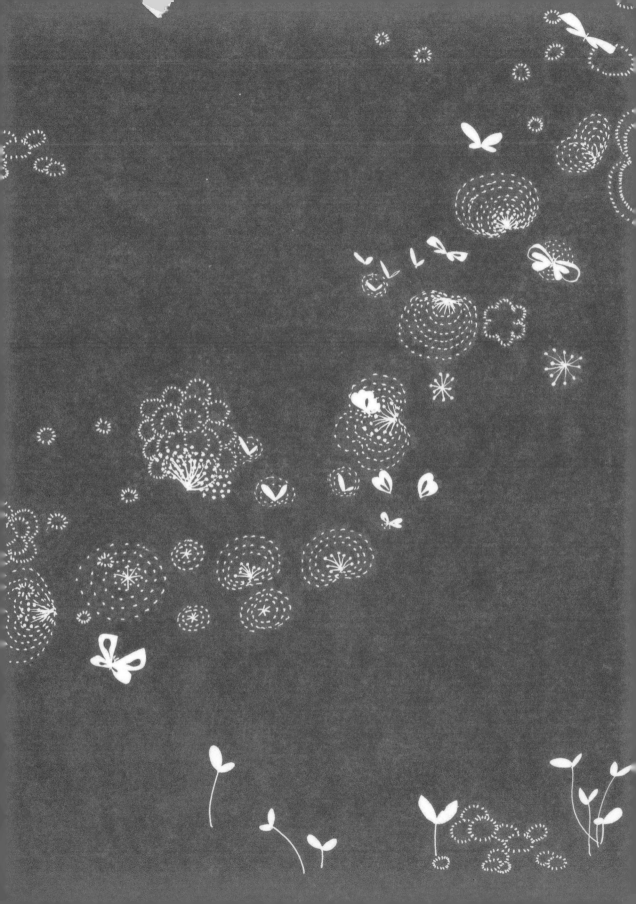